# Dear Parent:

Congratulations! Your child is taking the first steps on an exciting journey. The destination? Independent reading!

**STEP INTO READING®** will help your child get there. The program offers five steps to reading success. Each step includes fun stories and colorful art. There are also Step into Reading Sticker Books, Step into Reading Math Readers, Step into Reading Phonics Readers, Step into Reading Write-In Readers, and Step into Reading Phonics Boxed Sets—a complete literacy program with something to interest every child.

## Learning to Read, Step by Step!

**Ready to Read  Preschool–Kindergarten**
• big type and easy words • rhyme and rhythm • picture clues
For children who know the alphabet and are eager to begin reading.

**Reading with Help  Preschool–Grade 1**
• basic vocabulary • short sentences • simple stories
For children who recognize familiar words and sound out new words with help.

**Reading on Your Own  Grades 1–3**
• engaging characters • easy-to-follow plots • popular topics
For children who are ready to read on their own.

**Reading Paragraphs  Grades 2–3**
• challenging vocabulary • short paragraphs • exciting stories
For newly independent readers who read simple sentences with confidence.

**Ready for Chapters  Grades 2–4**
• chapters • longer paragraphs • full-color art
For children who want to take the plunge into chapter books but still like colorful pictures.

**STEP INTO READING®** is designed to give every child a successful reading experience. The grade levels are only guides. Children can progress through the steps at their own speed, developing confidence in their reading, no matter what their grade.

Remember, a lifetime love of reading starts with a single step!

# TALES FROM
# BEAR COUNTRY

Visit us on the Web!
StepIntoReading.com
www.randomhouse.com/kids
BerenstainBears.com

Educators and librarians, for a variety of teaching tools, visit us at
www.randomhouse.com/teachers

ISBN: 978-0-375-97232-4

Printed in the United States of America

10 9 8 7 6 5 4 3

# STEP INTO READING

## The Berenstain Bears
## TALES FROM
## BEAR COUNTRY

Step 1 and Step 2 Books

A Collection of Early Readers

## The Berenstains

Random House New York

# Contents

STEP INTO READING®

STEP 1

# The Berenstain Bears
# BIG BEAR

## SMALL BEAR

## The Berenstains

Random House 🏠 New York

Big bear.

Small bear.

Small hat,
big head.

Big hat,
small head.

Too small.

Too big.

Just right!

Just right!

One big.

One small.

Small suit,
big bear.

Big suit,

small bear.

Too tight.

Too loose.

Just right!

Just right!

One big.

One small.

Big bear,

small seat.

Small bear,
big seat.

Too heavy.

Too light.

Just right!
Just right!

One big.

One small.

Small bowl,
big bear.

Big bowl,
small bear.

Too little.

Too much.

Big bowl,

big bear.

Small bowl,

small bear.

Just right!

Just right!

# STEP INTO READING

## The Berenstain Bears

# BY THE SEA

## The Berenstains

Random House New York

Is it far,
Papa Bear?

Those seagulls mean
we'll soon be there.

There is the house
where we will stay.
Our shore vacation
starts today!

The wind was strong.
It opened the door.
Sand blew in
upon the floor!
This house was empty
for a while.
Each room has
its own sand pile.

Let's put on suits
and go in the water.

Not yet, son!
Not yet, daughter!

We must clean up,
room by room.
Here's a dustpan.
Here's a broom.

Now the clean-up
job is done.

It's time to have
some ocean fun.

Not just yet!
There's more to be done
before you start
your ocean fun.

There are

things to carry,

beds to make,

closets to clean,

walks to rake.

Mama, all of
that is done.
<u>Now</u> may we start
our ocean fun?

May we? May we?
May we, please,
dip our tootsies
in the seas?

Will you please relax!
You've got all day.
The ocean will
not go away.

There are many things
we must unpack.
Then we'll have
our little snack.

Mama, our little
snack is done.
<u>Now</u> may we start
our ocean fun?

Dears, it's much
too soon after food.

# Rats and phooey!

# Now, let's not be rude!

It's long after snacks.
May we go in soon?
It's getting late
in the afternoon!

That's why we're here,
to swim in the ocean.
But first, my dears,
let's put on some lotion.

# At last we can go into the water!

Wait, my son!

Wait, my daughter!

But, Papa! Will we never swim in the sea?

Relax! I just wanted you
to wait for me.

# Come on, cubs!
# Shake a leg!

Last one in
is a rotten egg!

The ocean is fun!
The ocean is great!
It may even have been
worth the wait!

# The Berenstain Bears

# CATCH THE BUS

## A TELL THE TIME STORY

The Berenstains

Random House New York

**6:59**

It is almost seven,

as you can see.

All is quiet

in the Bears'

Home Sweet Tree.

7:00

The cubs are asleep

at seven o'clock.

The alarm goes off.

It is quite a shock.

**7:05**

Five minutes later,
they are back to sleep.
Brother and Sister
are back to sleep!

Papa's coffee
starts to perk.
Papa will soon
be going to work.

And off to work
goes Grizzly Gus,
the driver of
the cubs' school bus.

**7:20**

The school bus starts

on its way

to pick up cubs

for school today.

7:25

What about Brother
and Sister Bear?
Will they be ready
when Gus gets there?

7:30

The bus stops here.

The bus stops there.

It picks up bear

after bear after bear.

Will our cubs be ready?

It is a worry.

They may not be—

unless they hurry.

7:35

But are <u>they</u> worrying?

They are not.

Are they hurrying?

They are not.

**7:40**

Gus picks up Bob
and Liz and Fred.
<u>Are</u> Brother and Sister
still in bed?

**7:45**

Ma sees the bus.

She starts to worry.

To catch that bus,

her cubs must hurry.

But upstairs there is not
a single sound—
the cubs are not even
up and around!

No more dreams
for Sister and Brother.
They wake up to
an angry mother.

The old school bus is
almost there—
at the house of
Brother and Sister Bear!

7:50

7:55

**7:56**

Hurry! Hurry!

Rush! Rush! Rush!

**7:57**

Wash and dress.

Comb and brush.

94

Downstairs! Downstairs in a flash!

Eat some breakfast! Off you dash!

At eight o'clock,
they catch the bus
and say hello
to Grizzly Gus!

Moral:

If you sleep past seven,
you might be late
when the school bus comes
for you at eight!

# The Berenstain Bears
# GO UP AND DOWN

## A Math Reader

## The Berenstains

Random House  New York

One bear going up.

Two bears coming down.

Three bears going up.

Four bears coming down.

One bear coming
down the UP.

Two bears going

up the DOWN.

Three bears coming
down the UP.

Four bears going
up the DOWN.

# Ten bears up—

UP

all piled up.

Ten bears down—

all piled up.

# Ten bears up.

# Ten bears down.

"Let's do it again!"

say both groups of ten.

"STOP! STOP!"

says a cop.

Twenty bears
all lined up.

# The Berenstain Bears RIDE THE THUNDERBOLT

## The Berenstains

Random House New York

# The Thunderbolt!

# Waiting in line.

# Buying tickets.

# Getting on.

Buckling up.

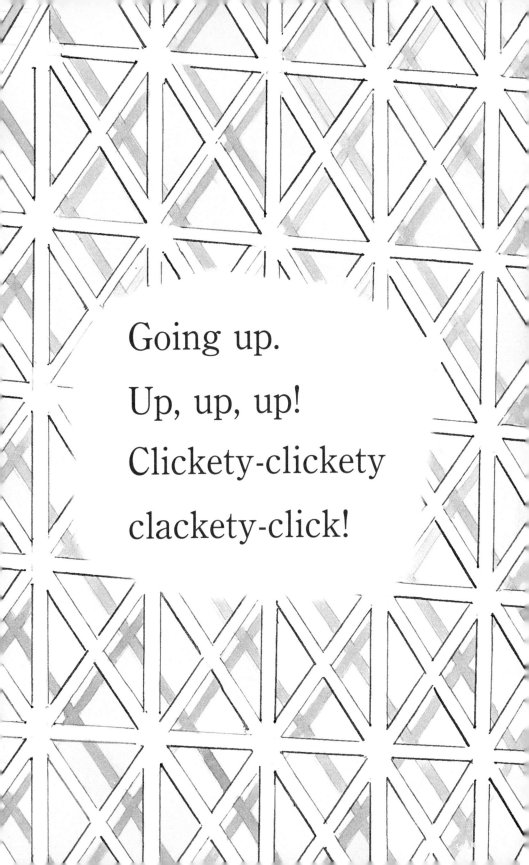

Going up.

Up, up, up!

Clickety-clickety

clackety-click!

At the top.

Going down.

Down, down, down!

Clackety-clackety

clickety-clack!

# Down and around!

Upside down!

# Into the dark!

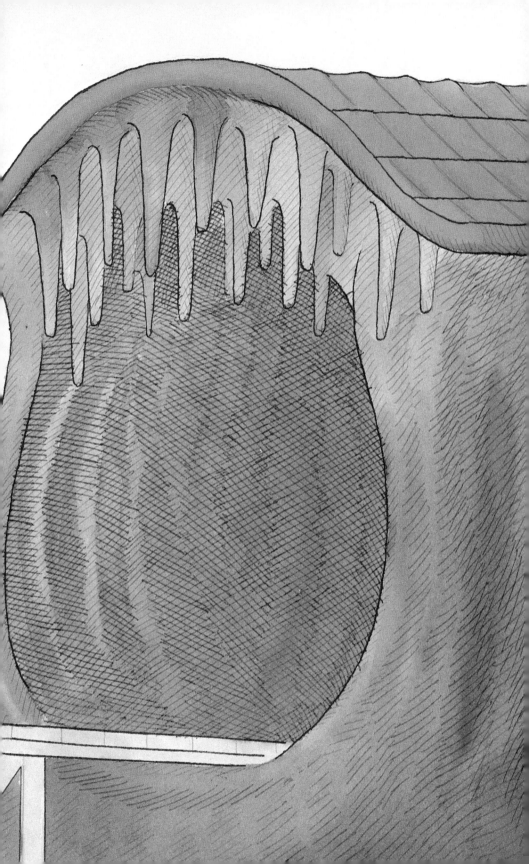

# Into the light.

Slowing down.

# Getting off.

"Again! Again! Do it again!"

"Not so quick!
Not so quick!
Your papa looks
a little sick."

"But that was fun!
That was fun!"

Going on again,
minus one.

STEP INTO READING®

STEP 1

# The Berenstain Bears

# We Like Kites

## The Berenstains

Random House 🏠 New York

A windy hill,
a summer sky,

a perfect day

for kites to fly.

# Running, running down the hill.

Will our kite fly?

Yes! It will!

More string!

More string!

Let out more string!

We catch the wind!
Our kites take wing!

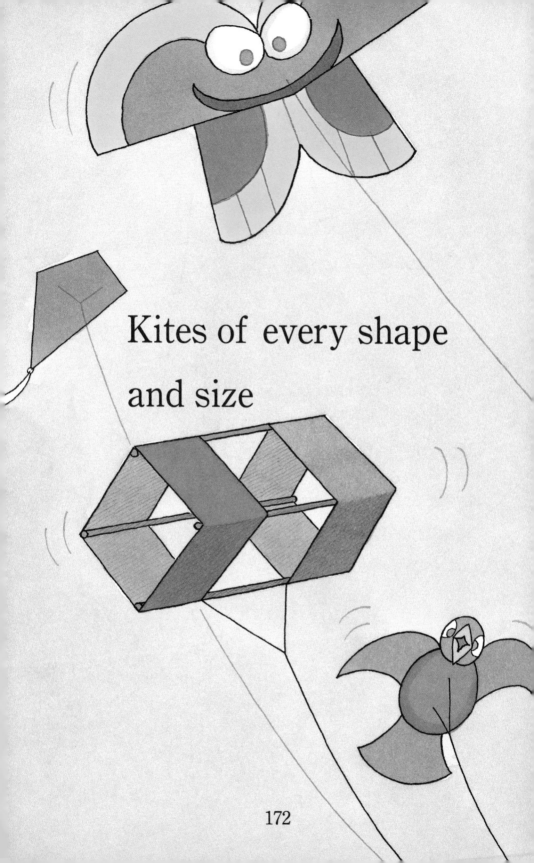

Kites of every shape
and size

dance across

the summer skies.

Some spin.

Some swoop.

Some loop the loop.

Sad kite, glad kite,

bat kite, cat kite.

A kite with stripes,

a kite with stars,

a kite that wants to
go to Mars.

A fire-breathing
dragon kite
gives the other kites
a fright.

The setting sun
says goodbye.

We reel in our kites
from up on high.

We head for home.
But that's okay.

The hill and sky
are here to stay.

And tomorrow is
another day.